JF
TRI Tripp, Vale
Molly's A+

MOLLY'S A+ PARTNER

BY VALERIE TRIPP

ILLUSTRATIONS NICK BACKES

VIGNETTES NICK BACKES, PHILIP HOOD

THE AMERICAN GIRLS COLLECTION®

Published by Pleasant Company Publications
Previously published in *American Girl*® magazine
Copyright © 2002 by Pleasant Company
All rights reserved. No part of this book may be used or reproduced in any manner whatsoever without written permission except in the case of brief quotations embodied in critical articles and reviews.
For information, address: Book Editor, Pleasant Company Publications, 8400 Fairway Place, P.O. Box 620998, Middleton, WI 53562.

Visit our Web site at **americangirl.com**

Printed in Singapore.
02 03 04 05 06 07 08 09 TWP 10 9 8 7 6 5 4 3 2 1

The American Girls Collection® and logo, American Girls Short Stories,™ the American Girl logo, Molly,® and Molly McIntire® are trademarks of Pleasant Company.

Library of Congress Cataloging-in-Publication Data

Tripp, Valerie, 1951–
Molly's A+ partner / by Valerie Tripp ; illustrations, Nick Backes ; vignettes, Nick Backes, Philip Hood.
p. cm. — (The American girls collection)
Summary: Nine-year-old Molly and her friend Susan have different ideas about how to present their school report on George Washington. Includes historical notes on George Washington and a recipe for cherry-nut cupcakes.

ISBN 1-58485-483-9
[1. Homework—Fiction. 2. Friendship—Fiction.
3. Washington, George, 1732–1799—Fiction.]
I. Backes, Nick, ill. II. Hood, Philip, ill. III. Title. IV. Series.
PZ7.T7363 Mot 2002 [Fic]—dc21 2001036374

OTHER AMERICAN GIRLS
SHORT STORIES:

FELICITY DISCOVERS A SECRET

JUST JOSEFINA

KIRSTEN AND THE CHIPPEWA

ADDY STUDIES FREEDOM

SAMANTHA'S BLUE BICYCLE

KIT'S HOME RUN

Picture Credits

The following individuals and organizations have generously given permission to reprint illustrations contained in "Looking Back": p. 30—Classroom, L3.2/p117, Minnesota Historical Society; Washington, © Geoffrey Clements/CORBIS; p. 31—Lincoln, North Wind Picture Archives; Roosevelt, © Bettmann/CORBIS; p. 32—Cannon, © Lee Snider, Lee Snider/CORBIS; Cannonballs, Arkansas Department of Parks and Tourism, photo by Chuck Haralson; p. 34—*Washington Crossing the Delaware,* Emanuel Leutze, 1851, The Metropolitan Museum of Art, gift of John Stewart Kennedy, 1897 (97.34), photo © 1992, The Metropolitan Museum of Art; p. 37—North Wind Picture Archives; p. 39—© CORBIS; p. 40—Photography by Jamie Young.

TABLE OF CONTENTS

MOLLY'S FAMILY AND FRIENDS

MOLLY'S A+ PARTNER 1

MEET THE AUTHOR 28

LOOKING BACK 29

MAKE CHERRY-NUT CUPCAKES 40

MOLLY'S FAMILY

DAD

Molly's father, a doctor who is somewhere in England, taking care of wounded soldiers.

MOM

Molly's mother, who holds the family together while Dad is away.

MOLLY

A nine-year-old who is growing up on the home front in America during World War Two.

JILL

Molly's fourteen-year-old sister, who is always trying to act grown-up.

RICKY

Molly's twelve-year-old brother—a big pest.

. . . AND FRIENDS

BRAD
Molly's five-year-old brother—a little pest.

LINDA
One of Molly's best friends, a practical schemer.

SUSAN
Molly's other best friend, a cheerful dreamer.

MISS CAMPBELL
Molly's teacher, who keeps her third-graders on their toes.

Molly's A+ Partner

"Susan, this is the best report anyone has ever done!" said Molly happily. "I bet we'll get an A+."

"Yes!" agreed Susan as she wrote her name in fancy script on the cover of the report. "I'm so glad we did George Washington and not Abraham Lincoln, like Linda and Alison. I always think that tall hat Lincoln wore looks so silly."

Molly chuckled. She didn't see what Lincoln's hat had to do with anything, but it didn't matter. Their report was finished, and she was very pleased with it.

All the students in Miss Campbell's class were doing reports on Washington or Lincoln to celebrate their February birthdays. Molly and Susan were partners, and they had worked very, very hard.

First, they'd marched straight to the library with sharpened pencils, clean white paper, and a special folder neatly labeled "Our Report." Molly read about Washington in the "W" volume of the encyclopedia, and Susan read about him in the "P" volume, under "Presidents." They read books from the biography section, too.

First, they'd marched straight to the library with sharpened pencils, clean white paper, and a special folder neatly labeled "Our Report."

They took notes, and met every day for a week to put their notes together.

When they wrote their first draft, they were careful to write in full sentences, to recheck the facts, and to look up all the hard words in the dictionary. Then Molly copied over the first half of the report in her best handwriting, and Susan copied over the second half. Today at Molly's house they had made a wonderful cover with a drawing of Washington's home, Mount Vernon, on it.

"I'm glad we're partners," Molly said as she signed her name on the cover under Susan's. Both she and Susan felt sorry for Linda. Not that

Alison wasn't nice! It was just that, as Molly went on to say, "It's so lucky when your partner is also one of your good friends."

"Mmm-hmm," Susan murmured vaguely. She was twirling a lock of her hair and staring at a painting in a big art book from the library. "I've been thinking," said Susan, looking up from the book. "You know what would be neat? Instead of just reading our report the way everyone else does, you and I could do something completely different."

"Like what?" asked Molly.

"Well, we could dress up and act out scenes from Washington's life," said Susan. She held up the book to show

Molly. "See? We could make wigs and capes, and—"

"Oh, Susan," said Molly. "I don't think so." Privately, she was horrified. She thought Susan's idea was perfectly terrible! Make wigs? Wear capes? First of all, it was too difficult. Secondly, everyone would laugh! Molly would die of embarrassment to stand up in front of the class in a wig and pretend to be the first president of the United States! "That isn't how you're supposed to present a report," she said. "You're supposed to stand up in your regular clothes and read it aloud to the class."

"Boring," said Susan, pretending to yawn. "Nothing to look at."

"What if we made a timeline showing the most important dates in Washington's life?" suggested Molly.

"That's the kind of thing everyone always does," protested Susan.

"Because that's what you're *supposed* to do," said Molly.

"Then ours will be different," said Susan.

"Then ours will be terrible!" said Molly.

Susan looked stubborn.

Molly sighed. "Listen, Susan. I don't want to do any acting out. I just want to read."

"How about this?" said Susan. "You read, and then you stop at certain points and I'll act something out."

"Well," said Molly slowly. "I *guess* that'll be okay."

"Good!" said Susan. "Then at the end maybe you and I can sing 'Yankee Doodle' together or something."

"*No,*" said Molly flatly. "No singing."

"Okay," said Susan, shrugging, holding up both hands. She grinned at Molly.

"Don't look so worried. It'll be fine. Really it will."

But Molly couldn't help feeling worried. She was going to present her report with a partner who wore a costume and sang? What had Susan lured her into?

As the days went by, Molly worried more and more. And she began to feel resentful of Susan, too. After all, as she was plugging away at making a timeline, which she was sure would earn them extra credit, Susan was wasting *her* time fussing around trying to make a tricorn hat, which would not earn them anything but teasing,

Molly was sure.

The reports were due Wednesday. Tuesday, after school, Molly and Susan met to practice their presentation for the next day. Molly showed Susan the timeline.

"Very nice," said Susan.

Molly's feelings were slightly hurt. She had worked long and hard on her timeline, and she thought Susan should be more enthusiastic. "I notice you didn't bring a costume," she said. "Does that mean you're not going to do that dressing up stuff?"

"Of course I am!" said Susan.

"Then," said Molly sharply, "where's your costume?"

"I couldn't bring it," said Susan. "The cape belongs to my mother, and she didn't want me dragging it all over the place and getting it dirty. And I can't move the hat and the wig because the glue is too wet."

Molly was nervous. "If I can't see your costume, can I at least hear what you're going to say?" she asked.

"Sure!" said Susan. "I've planned it very carefully." She opened the report. "I'll draw stars in the margins. Whenever you come to a star, stop reading because I'm going to stand up and act something out."

"Okay," said Molly as Susan drew the stars. "Tell me what you're going to do at the first star."

"Oh, it'll be great!" said Susan, all smiles. "I'm going to pretend that I'm

Washington when he was a boy." She stood up to show Molly. "I'm going to pretend to swing an axe, and watch the cherry tree as it falls, and—"

"Just a second!" Molly interrupted, sputtering. "I don't think you should do that cherry tree thing, Susan! Everyone knows it's probably not true."

"But that's not the point," said Susan. "I'm going to say—"

Molly interrupted again. "Please don't do it, Susan!" she begged. "Everyone will laugh! And Miss Campbell will think we didn't check our facts! I couldn't stand it! Not after all my hard work!"

"*Your* hard work?" said Susan.

"I worked hard, too. I'm your partner, remember?"

Humph! Some partner! thought Molly. *Fussing around wasting time on a silly hat!* She said quickly, "I'm just afraid it's going to make us look dumb."

"Dumb?!" exclaimed Susan, her cheeks pink with anger. "Well! If that's the way you feel about it, then I'm not going to tell you the other things I planned to say. I'm going home!"

"Wait!" wailed Molly as Susan stood up. "You can't go!"

But it was too late. The door slammed. Susan was gone.

That night, when Molly's mom came up to tuck her into bed, Molly was wide awake and fretting. "What's the matter?" asked Mom.

Molly sat up. "Susan and I had a fight about our report," she said. "Susan wants to act out parts of it, which I really, really don't like. And she's wasted a lot of time fussing over costumes and stuff that I think is useless. Then today, when she started to tell me what she was going to do, I got upset and she got mad and stormed off."

Mom sighed. "Partnerships can be hard," she said. "Especially when the partners have different ways of doing things."

Mom sighed. "Partnerships can be hard," she said. "Especially when the partners have different ways of doing things."

"Susan hasn't been a good partner on this report at all," grumbled Molly.

"She worked as hard as you did on the written part of the report, didn't she?" asked Mom.

"Yes," Molly grudgingly admitted.

"And she's been a good friend for a long time, too," added Mom. "I do think it would be too bad if your partnership ended your friendship." She kissed Molly's forehead. "Now try to get some sleep. Goodnight."

After Mom left, Molly thought about what she'd said. *Mom's right,* she decided. *Susan is a good friend even if she isn't a good partner. Tomorrow I'll tell Susan I'm sorry about the fight.*

Molly went to sleep feeling better, even though she was still sure she was heading toward one of the most embarrassing days of her life.

"Who would like to go first?" asked Miss Campbell the next day.

Linda and Alison shot their hands up, and Miss Campbell chose them to begin.

Molly leaned her chin on her hands and listened as Linda read aloud. Once in a while, Alison held up a picture to illustrate what Linda was reading. *Just exactly the way you're supposed to present a report,* Molly thought wistfully. *Wait'll they get a load of Susan!* She sighed, and remembered her decision to apologize.

Carefully, she slipped a note to Susan.

Susan smiled and sent a note back.

Molly read Susan's note. "Me, too," she said to herself.

"Very nice!" said Miss Campbell when Linda and Alison were done. "You girls worked hard, and you've given us a good, solid report. Molly and Susan, you can go next."

With a sinking heart, Molly went forward. She tacked up her timeline and stood next to Miss Campbell's desk. Susan was crouched behind the desk with her costume in a bag.

Molly began to read: "George Washington, The Father of Our Country. George Washington was born on February 22, 1732." Molly pointed to the beginning of her timeline, and the class murmured appreciatively. *I knew the timeline was a good idea!* Molly thought.

She continued reading: "Washington's father was a wealthy planter. George grew up . . . " As she read, Molly could hear Susan rattling around, putting on her costume. All too soon, Molly came to the first star, which marked the point where she was supposed to stop reading. She stopped. *Here goes!* she thought, bracing herself for giggles.

Susan stood up with a dramatic flourish.

"Oooohh!" gasped all the students admiringly. Molly looked. Her jaw dropped in amazement.

Susan's costume was fantastic! She had a big, sweeping black cape and tall black boots. She'd tucked her pants into the boots to look like breeches. Best of all, on her head she wore a wig made out of cotton balls topped by a gorgeous tricorn hat that was edged in gold braid and decorated with a plume of feathers.

Susan spoke. "There's a story that says that when Washington was a boy, he chopped down his father's best cherry tree." Susan swung an invisible axe, held her hand above her eyes, and pretended to watch a tree fall. "When his father asked him about it, young George supposedly said, 'I did it, Father. I cannot tell a lie.' Well, we don't know if this story is true or not. But the story shows that Washington was famous for being honest, and that's why people trusted him. And the story is also why we have cherry pie on his birthday!"

All the kids laughed and clapped.

Hey, they sort of like this, Molly realized. She went back to reading from the report, pointing to her timeline whenever she mentioned an important date. "George Washington was a famous soldier," she read. "He was the leader of the army at the time of the American Revolution." She came to another star, so she stopped, and Susan spoke again.

"This is a famous painting of Washington crossing the Delaware River on Christmas night in 1776," said Susan. She held up an art book and showed the class the painting. "He'd mostly lost battles till then, but in this painting he's on his way to surprise and, though he doesn't know it, defeat the British Army. The painting shows him standing up in the boat like this." Susan struck a proud pose. "Well, he probably would have fallen overboard if he really had stood up in the boat like that! But I think the artist wanted to show that Washington

Susan struck a proud pose.

was brave, and that's why his soldiers felt good about following him."

"Ahh," said the class, with understanding.

Boy, they really like this, Molly thought.

She looked over at Susan and grinned, and then she read again. She came to another star after she read, "During the harsh, cold winter of 1777, George Washington stayed with his soldiers at Valley Forge and suffered just as they did."

Susan had pulled on mittens and a scarf. She had sprinkled powder on her cape to look like snow, and she was carrying sticks of wood. "When Washington stayed with his men, it showed everyone that he was humble," she said. "He didn't act the way the king did. People knew he would be a good president because he would be a responsible leader who cared about them, like a father."

The class nodded and agreed.

Molly read to the end of the report: "And so you can see, George Washington was not only our first president, he was also one of our greatest presidents. That's why we call him the Father of Our Country."

Susan added, "George Washington will always be a well-loved president. You may not know it, but there is a verse about him in a song we all sing." Susan sang all by herself to the tune of "Yankee Doodle":

There was Captain Washington,
upon a slapping stallion,
A-giving orders to his men,
I guess there was a million.

Molly joined in with everyone else as Susan led them in the chorus:

Yankee Doodle, keep it up,
Yankee Doodle dandy!
Mind the music and the step,
And with the girls be handy!

"Hurray!" cheered the class. They clapped and stamped their feet and whistled.

"That was splendid!" exclaimed

Miss Campbell after the class quieted down. "Molly and Susan, you showed us how good partners work!" She beamed at the girls. "A+ for both of you," she said.

Molly smiled at Susan, and Susan grinned back. Susan's hat was tilted and her wig was askew, but she didn't look funny to Molly. She looked like a good friend—and a very good partner.

VALERIE TRIPP

At 9 Now

When my sister was in third grade, my father dressed up in a hooded fur parka, mukluks, and huge mittens to help a friend of hers present a report about Eskimos. What a good partner *he* was!

Valerie Tripp has written forty-four books in The American Girls Collection, including ten about Molly.

LOOKING
BACK
1944

A Peek Into the Past

FINDING HOPE IN THE PAST

George Washington

To celebrate the birthdays of past presidents Washington and Lincoln, Molly's class wrote reports, just as you might do today. For children on the home front during World War Two, remembering Washington and Lincoln was especially important. Both were

Abraham Lincoln

leaders during times of war in American history—Washington commanded the Continental Troops during the Revolutionary War, and Lincoln was president during the Civil War. And both led their followers to victory.

Remembering past victories gave Americans hope during World War Two. In a radio speech in 1942, President Roosevelt compared the crisis of World War Two to the struggle Americans faced during the Revolutionary War. Many people believed America would never win independence

Roosevelt gave frequent radio speeches.

from England, but Washington and the Continental Army proved them wrong. President Roosevelt assured Americans that though they again faced difficult times, victory would be theirs.

Molly and Susan's report touched on one of the most famous events of the Revolutionary War—Washington's crossing of the Delaware River on Christmas night, 1776. Until then, Washington had lost every major battle against the British. He had lost forts, gunpowder, and cannon—and especially men.

A Revolutionary War cannon

A soldier's meal: biscuits, hard cheese, and dried beef

The men who remained in Washington's army were cold, hungry, and discouraged. They had begun to lose faith in Washington, and some of his officers even whispered about replacing him.

The British now occupied New York City. They had declared the war over during the winter because of the bad weather and because they believed Washington's army was no longer a threat to them. The British officers were enjoying themselves, dining on the best food and wine and dancing in ballrooms.

Christmas night found Washington and his men on the bank of the Delaware River. Ice flowed by on the swift current. Sleet stung his face. Winds snared his cape.

Washington encouraged his troops as they struggled across the Delaware River.

His men had no shoes and were hungry. The horses were shoeless, too. They slipped in the ice as they pulled wagons loaded with cannon to the riverbank. The British might have stopped fighting for the winter, but Washington saw this night

as his last chance. He hoped to catch the enemy troops by surprise.

Across the river in Trenton, New Jersey, were Hessians (HESH-ens). They were soldiers from Germany, hired by King George to fight for England. If Washington could beat the Hessians, he might still win the war. If he failed, all might be lost. The mission's password showed how desperate Washington felt. It was "Liberty or Death."

A spy in Washington's camp wrote a note to the Hessian general in Trenton, telling him that Washington planned to attack at dawn the next day. But the general was attending a Christmas party. He did not want to be bothered. "They're half-naked," he said. "Let them come."

And come they did. At eight o'clock on December 26, after a long, cold night, Washington's troops marched into Trenton. Most of the Hessian soldiers were still in bed, recovering from the party the night before. By nine o'clock, Washington's Continental Army had

The surrender of the Hessians at the Battle of Trenton

taken the city and nearly a thousand Hessian prisoners. The Hessian general who had ignored the warning of Washington's attack died in battle that morning. In his pocket was the spy's folded, forgotten note. Washington's desperate mission had succeeded.

When the British in New York City learned of General Washington's victory, their celebration came to an end. But for Americans, the victory was cause for great celebration. Their confidence in Washington and in the country's ability to win the war was restored. Little did they know that more than 150 years later, Americans like Molly would once again take heart in Washington's victory as they waited for war to end.

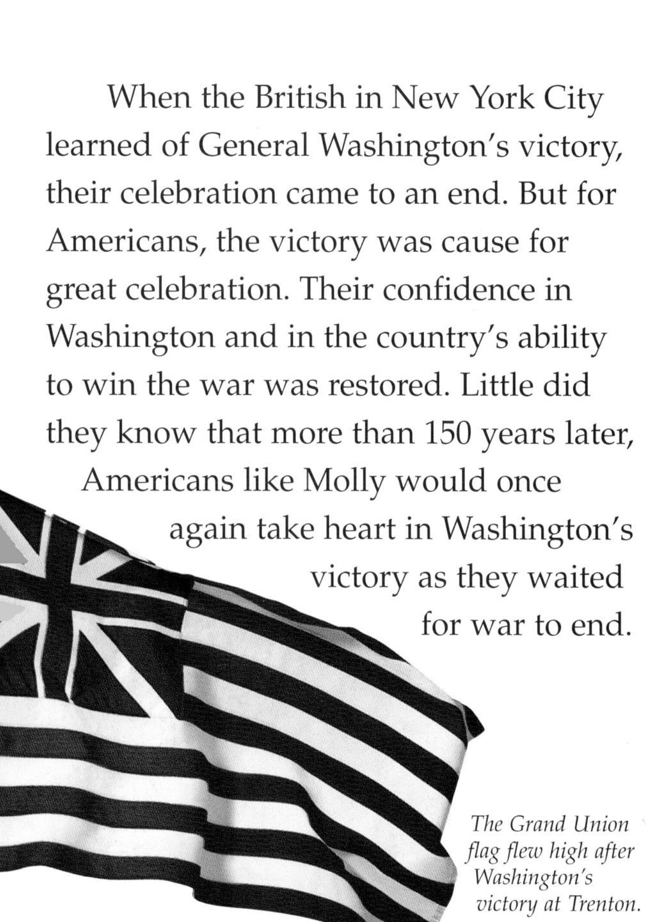

The Grand Union flag flew high after Washington's victory at Trenton.

By the 1940s, America's flag had changed, but the country's determination and enthusiasm for victory remained the same.

AN
AMERICAN
GIRLS
PASTIME

Make Cherry-Nut Cupcakes

Honor our first president with these cheery cherry cakes!

The story that Molly and Susan told their class about Washington cutting down his father's cherry tree comes from a book written after Washington died. The story is probably not true, but it shows that Washington was a good man who did what he thought was right. We can honor our first president with cherry desserts based on the story of the cherry tree. Bake these cupcakes for Presidents' Day—or any day!

You Will Need:

An adult to help you

Ingredients

2 1/2 cups flour, sifted

3 1/2 teaspoons baking powder

1/2 teaspoon salt

1/2 cup shortening

1 1/4 cups sugar

2 eggs

3/4 cup milk

1/4 cup cherry syrup (from jar of cherries)

3/4 teaspoon almond extract

1/2 cup finely chopped nuts

3/4 cup finely chopped maraschino cherries

Your favorite pink or white frosting

Equipment

Cupcake or muffin pans
16 paper cupcake liners
Sifter
Medium mixing bowl
Measuring cups and spoons
Large mixing bowl
Electric mixer
Rubber spatula
Wooden spoon
Potholders
Toothpick
Wire cooling racks
Butter knife

1. Preheat the oven to 350 degrees. Line the cupcake pans with paper liners.

2. Put the sifter into the medium mixing bowl. Measure the flour, baking powder, and salt into the sifter and sift them into the bowl.

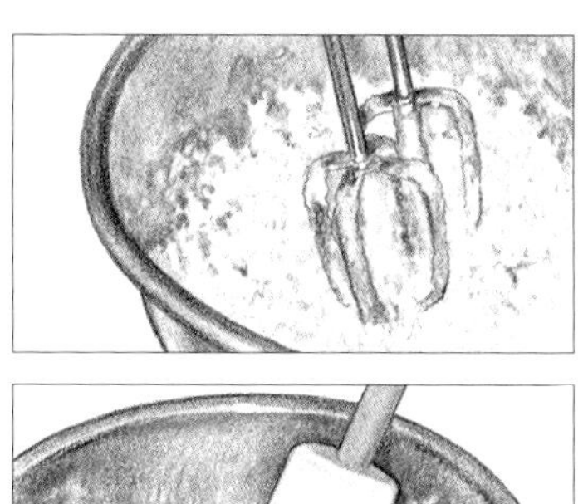

3. Measure the shortening and sugar into the large mixing bowl. Use the electric mixer to beat the mixture until fluffy. Add the eggs, and beat for one more minute. Use the rubber spatula to scrape down the sides of the bowl after beating.

4. Add the milk, the cherry syrup, the almond extract, and half of the dry ingredients to the shortening and sugar mixture. Beat well. Add the remaining dry ingredients, and beat again.

5. Use the wooden spoon to stir in the nuts and 1/2 cup of the cherries.

6. Spoon the batter into the cupcake liners until each is about 2/3 full.

7. Bake the cupcakes for 20 minutes. Use the potholders to remove the cupcakes from the oven.

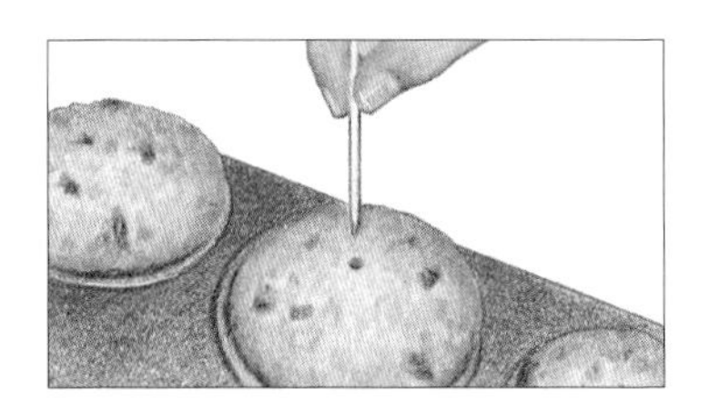

8. Poke a toothpick into the center of one cupcake. If the toothpick comes out clear the cupcakes are done. Set the cupcake pans on the racks to cool.

9. After 10 minutes, take the cupcakes out of the pans. Let them cool on the racks, then frost them using the butter knife. Use the remaining chopped cherries to decorate the cupcakes.